ONE WISH APIECE

"I wish to be tall," Tatty said suddenly, taking the lamp in her hands. She had been thinking about this all afternoon.

"But you *will* be tall when you get older," Phoebe said.

"I want to be tall *now.*"

All the girls watched Tatty closely, but she did not seem to get any taller.

"I've just thought of the most wonderful wish anybody could ever think of!" Phoebe said. She seized the lamp and held it high. "I wish to have an invisible cloak!" she announced.

Phoebe set the lamp on the floor and picked up the black velvet cape which lay beside her. With a grand gesture she swept it across her shoulders . . . and vanished from sight!

Miss Know It All and the Wishing Lamp

A Butterfield Square Story

by Carol Beach York

Illustrated by Leslie Morrill

A BANTAM SKYLARK BOOK®
TORONTO · NEW YORK · LONDON · SYDNEY · AUCKLAND

For my sister Gloria with love

RL 4, 008-012

MISS KNOW IT ALL AND THE WISHING LAMP
A Bantam Book / October 1987

ISBN 0-553-15536-9

Published simultaneously in the United States and Canada

Bantam Books are published by Bantam Books, Inc. Its trademark, consisting of the words "Bantam Books" and the por-
trayal of a rooster, is Registered in U.S. Patent and Trademark
Office and in other countries. Marca Registrada. Bantam
Books, Inc., 666 Fifth Avenue, New York, New York 10103.

PRINTED IN THE UNITED STATES OF AMERICA

S   0 9 8 7 6 5 4 3 2 1

Contents

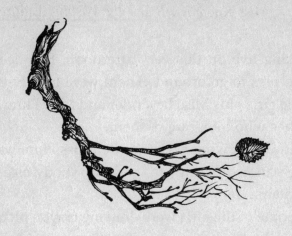

1
What Miss Lavender Found

It was late afternoon. Lights glowed in the windows of the sturdy brick houses of Butterfield Square. A cold end-of-October wind swept fallen leaves along the pavements. Nearly all the trees were bare. Winter was coming.

At Number 18, *The Good Day Orphanage For Girls*, a cozy fire burned in the parlor grate and a wonderful smell of pumpkin pies filled the hallways. It was the day before Halloween, just the right time of year for pumpkin pies. Cook was baking five on this very afternoon. She needed five pies to go around. There were twenty-eight little girls plus Miss Lavender and Miss Plum, the ladies who took care of them.

It was growing dark outside. Miss Plum was in the parlor drinking tea, and everybody else was upstairs.

Some of the girls were drawing crayon pictures of jack-o'-lantern faces for the jack-o'-lantern picture contest at school the next day.

There was also going to be a prize for the best costume, and some of the girls were trying on their costumes one last time. Other girls were still getting costumes ready, fussing around noisily with a big box of masks and odds and ends left over from other Halloweens.

Three girls were helping Miss Lavender clean out her closet: Tatty, Mary, and Little Ann.

Most people cleaned their closets in springtime, and it was called Spring Cleaning. Miss Lavender prefered October, although she had never said why. Miss Lavender didn't always do things exactly the way everybody else did. No one else had so many ruffles on her dresses or wore so many curls in her hair—or cleaned closets in October.

Tatty, Mary, and Little Ann had offered to help. They knew there would be many interesting things to see in Miss Lavender's closet.

"Here is a string of beads you may play with, Little Ann," Miss Lavender said, shuffling her plump fingers through a box of old jewelry. Little Ann was not much help cleaning closets because she was only five years old. She put on the string of beads and ran away to look at herself in a mirror.

"Tatty, please hand me that straw hat." Miss Lavender pointed toward a floppy yellow straw hat with a red paper poppy on the brim. "I think I will give that to the church rummage sale."

Tatty was a dark-eyed little girl with hair tumbling every which way and jam on her collar. She was more help than Little Ann, but she was not very tall. The brim of the hat was sticking out over the edge of the closet shelf. Tatty could see it easily enough, but she couldn't reach it. She stood on her tiptoes and stretched her arm as high as she could stretch. But she couldn't reach the hat.

"I'll get it," Mary said helpfully.

Mary was nine, two years older than Tatty and two years taller. She had curly red hair and three hundred and eleven freckles. Miss Know It All had told her so, and Miss Know It All knew everything. Besides her freckles, Mary was famous at *The Good Day Orphanage For Girls* for writing poems.

> *Halloween! Halloween!*
> *What will I wear?*
> *Who will I spook?*
> *Who will I scare?*

That was Mary's Halloween poem. She also had poems for Valentine's Day and Christmas and Fourth of July.

Mary had to stand on tiptoe too, but she could reach the hat. Tatty sighed and tugged up a drooping stocking. The straw hat was the third thing Miss Lavender had asked Tatty to hand to her that Tatty hadn't been able to reach.

Mary admired the red paper poppy, and then she plopped the hat on her head. It didn't have to go to the rummage sale *this very minute*.

What Miss Lavender Found

Just as Miss Lavender was taking an old black velvet cape from the back of the closet, where she kept the things she hardly ever wore anymore, a girl named Phoebe came along, trying to think of a Halloween costume she could make. She had thought of a hundred marvelous costumes, but she hadn't found the things she needed to make them: Wings for a dragon. A diamond crown for a queen. Fangs for a horrible werewolf. A lion skin, or a real pirate sword. None of these important items were anywhere around *The Good Day*. The moment she saw Miss Lavender's black velvet cape, Phoebe knew she had her costume.

"Oh, Miss Lavender!" Phoebe almost knocked over Little Ann, who was coming back from the mirror with her beads. "Can I borrow your cape for my Halloween costume? Oh, please, please, *please?*"

Phoebe threw herself on her knees and held up her hands in prayer. She liked to be dramatic, and everybody was used to her. They all went on with their own business. Little Ann wriggled around Phoebe and began to look in the jewelry box for more beads. Tatty and Mary poked in the pockets

of a discarded skirt to see if there was anything to be found.

"I could be a bat if I had that cape. Oh, please, Miss Lavender, please, please, *please!*"

Miss Lavender hardly heard. She had opened a worn-looking cardboard box she had found at the very back of the closet, and she was looking inside the box with a surprised expression. "Why, look what I've found," she said, and Tatty peered around Miss Lavender's elbow to look into the box.

"Please, please, *please!*" Phoebe went on and on, but nobody was listening.

"It's the wishing lamp," Miss Lavender continued. From the worn old cardboard box she took out a small brass lamp—an old-fashioned Aladdin's lamp.

"A wishing lamp?" Mary looked out from under the brim of the straw hat, and Little Ann lifted her head from the jewelry box. Even Phoebe was silent now.

"Can you make a wish with it?" Tatty looked at the lamp curiously. "Wishes that come true?"

Miss Lavender was smiling to herself. "After all

these years—why, I'd forgotten all about this lamp."

"Let's make some wishes," Mary said. She felt very excited to think they had discovered a real true wishing lamp. She had always wanted one.

"First let's show Miss Plum," Miss Lavender suggested. She put the lamp carefully back into the cardboard box and closed the closet door—which started Phoebe off again.

Phoebe fell to her knees. "Please, Miss Lavender, please, please, *please!*"

Miss Lavender opened the door again and handed out the black velvet cape. "Yes, dear," she said, "you may borrow the cape for your Halloween costume. Then we'll give it to the rummage sale."

"I'm Bat Lady," Phoebe cried with glee, throwing the cape across her shoulders with a flourish and lifting her arms like bat wings.

Down they went to the parlor then to show Miss Plum the wishing lamp. Miss Lavender, Tatty, Little Ann with all her beads, Mary under the straw hat, and Phoebe the Bat Lady swooping behind.

2
The Wishing Lamp

Miss Plum was still in the parlor drinking tea. She was as tall and thin as Miss Lavender was short and plump. She had no ruffles on her dresses and no curls in her hair. She was neat and plain with a bun of gray hair and sensible shoes. She always knew the right thing to do and the right thing to say to make the little girls at *The Good Day* happy. They all thought she was very beautiful, even without the ruffles and curls.

Miss Plum was looking into the fireplace,

admiring the glowing red and yellow flames and feeling drowsy, the way looking at glowing flames always made her feel. When she heard the sound of footsteps (and bat wings), she roused herself and turned toward the doorway.

In came Miss Lavender with the cardboard box, Mary with her straw hat, Little Ann with beads, and Tatty—who Miss Plum could quickly see was a little less perfect than she could be, needing a comb for her hair and a pair of stockings that stayed up.

What Miss Plum was not prepared to see was a swishing, swooshing bat and a magic wishing lamp. Until now, it had been a quiet, ordinary afternoon.

"I'm Bat Lady." Phoebe flapped her cape and pretended to fly around the room. It made Miss Plum dizzy just to watch.

"We found a magic wishing lamp," Tatty burst out with the news. She climbed on the sofa and sank down on her knees beside Miss Plum.

"I want to wish," Little Ann begged, reaching up to catch hold of the box Miss Lavender carried. Miss Lavender patted Little Ann's soft yellow hair and said, "Just a moment, Little Ann. We must show Miss Plum first."

Miss Plum made room for Little Ann on the sofa, and she climbed up beside Tatty.

"Let's all be quiet," Miss Plum said hopefully. She meant Phoebe, because everybody else was already quiet. Bat Lady fluttered to a stop at last and settled in a black velvet heap on the carpet by the fireplace.

Miss Lavender sat in a chair by the sofa and put the box on her lap. Then she lifted out the wishing lamp. The brass gleamed in the firelight, golden and mysterious, like something that came from ancient days long ago.

"Look at what I found in the back of my closet." Miss Lavender held the lamp a moment and then passed it over to Miss Plum. "I'd forgotten about it long ago, forgotten that I still had it."

Mary didn't see how anybody could forget they had a wishing lamp!

"What a pretty little thing," Miss Plum said, turning the lamp this way and that. Lamplight reflected on the brass, and Little Ann put out a finger to touch.

"Years ago, when I was about as big as —" Miss Lavender looked around at the girls thoughtfully— "about as big as Tatty, my sister and I sent away for this wishing lamp. We saw an advertisement in a magazine and we sent away for it. We thought it would *never* come. Every day we watched for the mailman. I thought I was going to be all grown up before the lamp ever came."

All the little girls giggled. Phoebe rustled her cape. It was getting too hot by the fireside, but she didn't want to take off her wonderful costume.

"Finally the lamp arrived. And there were instructions." Miss Lavender remembered this all of a sudden. "Yes, instructions—now let's see if I still have them." She looked into the cardboard box, and sure enough, there was a small slip of paper at the bottom of the box. The paper was old and brittle. It crinkled in her fingers as she carefully unfolded it. She read aloud from the crinkly paper.

Congratulations. You have just purchased a Wonder Year Wishing Lamp. Your lamp will give one hundred and one wishes. One wish per person.

One hundred and one wishes sounded like a lot—but only one wish per person? Mary had already thought of *many* wishes she wanted to make. Miss Lavender continued reading from the slip of paper.

Instructions: Simply hold the lamp firmly in both hands and say your wish. Speak clearly. The magic lamp will grant your wish.

When Miss Lavender finished reading the instructions she said, "My sister and I had so much fun. And all our friends, too. We took the lamp to school one day and everybody had a wish."

"Isn't that nice," Miss Plum said cheerfully. "A hundred and one wishes, plenty to share."

"How many are left?" Tatty asked solemnly. If Miss Lavender and her sister had let everybody at school make a wish, maybe the wishes were all used up.

"Oh, I suppose they are all gone now." Miss Lavender winked at Miss Plum.

"Ha, ha, ha." A voice spoke from the doorway.

Everybody turned and looked toward the doorway. There stood Elsie May, the oldest *Good Day* girl. She had two long yellow braids tied with ribbon, and she thought she was the best and prettiest and smartest of all the *Good Day* girls. Mostly she was just the bossiest.

Elsie May's nose was stuck into the air to show how silly she thought a magic wishing lamp was. "That's just pretend," she scoffed, twiddling the end of one of her braids.

"It is not!" Phoebe shouted. "Why don't you go away."

"Phoebe, Phoebe," Miss Plum scolded gently. "Don't be rude."

Phoebe huddled in her cape and scowled at Elsie May.

Tatty and Little Ann looked at the lamp. Was it only pretend? Mary looked at the lamp too; she had lots of wishes all ready to go. She wanted yellow hair instead of red. She wanted a blue dress made of silk. She wanted a new book to write her poems in and an umbrella all her own. Winter was coming. Soon it would snow. Mary wanted ice skates and a sled and a pair of pink mittens. It was bad enough to think that the lamp granted only one wish to each person, and now here was Elsie May saying it was only pretend, not a real magic lamp at all.

"I think—" Miss Plum began, but whatever it was she was thinking nobody ever knew, for just then a loud slamming sound was heard at the front door.

Bang, bang, bang.

No one in the whole world knocked like that except one person—Mr. Not So Much. Everyone around the parlor fireplace knew the sound of that knock.

Mr. Not So Much was on the Board of Directors of *The Good Day Orphanage For Girls*, and he came once a month to go over various matters with Miss Plum and Miss Lavender—mostly money matters. Mr. Not So Much thought money was all that *really* mattered anyway. He always found too much being spent at *The Good Day.* He was always telling Miss Lavender and Miss Plum, "Not so much wood on the fire. Not so much sugar in the tea. Not so much butter on the bread." But the ladies never listened, and every time he came, Mr. Not So Much had to say it all again.

Everyone dreaded his visits. No one more than poor Cook, who was now sure to be held to blame for baking five pumpkin pies in one single afternoon.

And there was no way she could hide this fact, for the spicy fragrance of pumpkin pies floated from the kitchen down the hallway at this very moment. It was the first thing Mr. Not So Much smelled as the door was opened and he stalked in out of the cold, dark October afternoon.

3
Mr. Not So Much

Cook herself was the one to open the door. She tried to shrink behind it so Mr. Not So Much would not see her.

Cook was as round and plump as Miss Lavender, so a lot of her still stuck out from behind the door, but Mr. Not So Much barged on down the hallway toward the parlor without a glance at her—much to Cook's relief.

Crayon drawings of jack-o'-lanterns decorated

the walls of the hallway, and Mr. Not So Much could immediately see that too much paper and crayon and sticky tape was being used at *The Good Day.* He smelled the pies too, of course. Money was surely being wasted here. It ran through the ladies' fingers like water, as always. He felt truly sorry that he had come. Visits to Number 18 Butterfield Square were as hard on him as they were on Miss Lavender and Miss Plum and Cook.

He glanced up the stairway as he passed by and saw small ghosts and goblins flitting along the upstairs hall. Three dreadful faces stared down at him between the upstairs railings: a witch with a great green wart on her chin, a fierce pirate with a patch over one eye, and a devil with red horns. But when Mr. Not So Much stared back, the three faces ran away, and it was only three little girls with their Halloween masks.

"Foolishness, foolishness," Mr. Not So Much mumbled to himself as he reached the parlor. He was a tall, skin-and-bones man with a long, bony face. His bony face was always stern. His overcoat was black as night.

No one in the parlor had moved since the sound

of that first heavy knock at the door. Phoebe sat covered with her too-warm black cape. Tatty and Little Ann were on the sofa beside Miss Plum, and Miss Lavender sat with the empty cardboard box in her lap.

Elsie May stood where she was like a stick, and the firelight gleamed on the wishing lamp Miss Plum was holding in her hands.

"What's this? What's this?" Mr. Not So Much saw the lamp at once. He was sure it was more foolishness, more money squandered.

No one answered his question.

Mr. Not So Much frowned at the warm, perspiring girl crouched by the fire in a big black cape. He never knew what the girls here would be up to next. He thought the girl by the fire looked feverish and should be put to bed. He set his gloves on a table, but he did not take off his coat or his hat.

This was a good sign, Miss Plum and Miss Lavender thought. It meant he would not stay long. When he took off his coat and hat, it meant he wanted to go over all the bills and he would fuss over every one. Sometimes Miss Lavender and Miss Plum forgot to listen when he fussed, they had heard it all so many times before.

"What's this, now?" Mr. Not So Much repeated crossly, and Miss Plum was jerked out of her trance.

"It's a lamp," she said. Because that did not seem quite enough to say, she added, "Miss Lavender sent away for it."

Ah, here was money being wasted indeed!

"Sent away for it?" Mr. Not So Much shifted his brooding eyes to Miss Lavender. "Sent away where? And why?"

Where? Why? Miss Lavender gathered her memories.

"It was an advertisement in a magazine—" she began.

The words were hardly out of her mouth before Mr. Not So Much threw up his hand in disapproval. *He* did not send away for strange things he saw advertised in magazines. How could you trust your money in the mails? How could you pay money for something you had not even seen? But he might have known Miss Lavender would have none of these practical concerns. She was just the one to fritter away money on things she saw in magazines. How many times had she done this, he wondered. He was beginning to get a headache.

"I sent for it a long time ago," Miss Lavender explained. "When I was a little girl."

Mr. Not So Much felt a little better when he heard that *Good Day* money had not been involved. Still, it was a foolish thing to do.

"It's a wishing lamp," Miss Lavender hastened to add. She could see that Mr. Not So Much did not approve of mail order, and she thought he might be more agreeable if he knew how special the brass lamp was supposed to be.

"Ah ha!" Now Mr. Not So Much's head was throbbing painfully. "Such foolishness, such miserable foolishness," he declared. All the little girls shrank back timidly.

"Ladies, you amaze me. Do you actually believe that lamp is—is"—Mr. Not So Much sputtered for words —"is magic?"

Finally he got it said, and everybody in the parlor jumped a little when he bellowed it out.

Cook, sneaking by in the hallway on her way to the kitchen, was so startled she clutched her apron and ran the rest of the way to the safety of the bright, warm kitchen where the five pumpkin pies were baking.

Miss Plum gestured vaguely. "Oh, perhaps not real magic," she started to say, but Mr. Not So Much wasn't listening.

"The best place for *that* is the wastebasket." He looked around to see if he could spot a wastebasket handy.

The girls stared at the lamp with dismay, and Tatty cried out, "Oh, no, don't throw the lamp away!"

There was a stunned silence in the parlor. None of the *Good Day* girls had ever shouted at Mr. Not So Much. It was not good manners to shout, and they were much too afraid of him anyway.

Mr. Not So Much was no less shocked than anyone else. He felt his head throbbing again. Before the ladies could apologize for Tatty's outburst, he snatched the lamp from Miss Plum and shoved it at the little girl with the tousled hair and frightened eyes.

"Take this out of my sight," he commanded. "Now off with you, all of you." He swung around to include Mary and Phoebe and Elsie May, and even a girl in a ghost-sheet who happened to be peeking in the parlor door.

The girls scattered like leaves in the wind. The black velvet cape dragged on the floor behind Phoebe, who forgot she was Bat Lady in her effort to get away from Mr. Not So Much.

Little Ann's beads broke and bounced around in every direction across the carpet. But she never looked back one time.

Tatty had the wishing lamp, and she ran fastest of all in case Mr. Not So Much should change his mind and want it back.

Even Elsie May hurried, though she pretended she was not one bit scared. Mary hung onto her hat as she ran, and the red paper poppy was the last thing to be seen going out the parlor door.

Mr. Not So Much left just after. The last thing he saw was a paper sign one of the girls had taped to the door:

A WITCH LIVES HEAR

"Fiddlesticks," he said, and he slammed the front door behind him.

In the parlor, Miss Lavender and Miss Plum noticed that Mr. Not So Much had forgotten his gloves.

"Fiddlesticks, indeed." Miss Lavender said. "He'll be coming back."

They sat in silence, waiting. But the next few minutes passed, and there was no loud banging at the door to announce Mr. Not So Much returning for his gloves.

They began to relax, sitting there in the fire-light. There was one last sip of tea (grown cold) in Miss Plum's cup.

"When you and your sister had the lamp," Miss Plum asked, sipping the last sip, "did you think your wishes really came true?"

"It's been such a long time," Miss Lavender mused. "Yes, I suppose we did think so. Or at least we liked to pretend we did. I do recall that my sister wished for a doll with eyes that would open and close, and that's just what she got for her next birthday."

"I wonder what the girls will wish for," Miss

Plum said thoughtfully. She was sure the girls were probably already in the midst of making wishes somewhere upstairs. "I hope they won't be disappointed."

"I wouldn't worry." Miss Lavender adjusted a ruffle on her skirt. "Just wishing is part of the fun, and who knows, perhaps some of their wishes will come true."

4
Wishing

As soon as the girls were out of the parlor, all fear of Mr. Not So Much vanished. They dashed toward the stairs, delirious with joy. Not only had they escaped Mr. Not So Much, they now had a wonderful magic wishing lamp.

They flew along the hall, past the potted fern and the umbrella stand, and up the stairway with its smooth, gleaming, dark banisters.

Tatty headed for her own room, and because she had the lamp, everybody thundered after her.

Tatty shared a room with Mary and Phoebe. There were three beds, each in a corner, and a round hooked rug in the middle of the floor. There was a table with three chairs beside it by the window. That was where Tatty and Mary and Phoebe did their schoolwork and painted pictures with a watercolor set Phoebe had and did other important things. Last summer, right at that very table, they had glued together one hundred and fifty-two Popsicle sticks and made a little house.

Yellow curtains hung at the windows, and a paper goblin Mary had made for Halloween dangled from the cord of a window shade. It was a very beautiful room.

So they were all at last safe in Tatty's room, breathless and pink with excitement. The girl in the sheet had come too, and when she pulled the sheet off over her head, there was tomboy Kate— the *Good Day* champion tree climber, fence walker, and cartwheel turner.

"I didn't know you were going to be a ghost for Halloween," Elsie May said when she saw Kate come out from under the sheet.

"I'm not," Kate said. "I'm still deciding. I want

to be something funny or something scary, but lots scarier than a ghost."

Elsie May sniffed. She didn't want to be funny *or* scary. She wanted to be pretty. She was going to be a gypsy princess. Her Halloween costume was a long skirt borrowed from Miss Plum and some bracelets Miss Lavender had given her. (Miss Lavender's supply of jewelry was without end.) Elsie May also had a peacock feather she was going to wear in her hair. Let other girls be hobos with knapsacks and sooty cheeks. Let them be silly bedsheet ghosts or devils with cardboard pitchforks. Elsie May was going to be a beautiful princess.

"Can we make wishes?" Little Ann tugged at Tatty's arm.

"Let's be orderly," Mary said. She felt in charge because she was wearing Miss Lavender's big straw hat. She closed the bedroom door and made everybody sit down in a circle on the hooked rug. Even Elsie May sat down. She thought the magic wishing lamp was silly, but if it really worked, she wanted to have a wish too.

Tatty put the lamp in the middle of the circle.

"Can I be first?" Little Ann begged.

Elsie May rolled her eyes to show she didn't agree, but Mary said yes, Little Ann could be first. All the other girls watched eagerly as Mary gave the wishing lamp to Little Ann.

"Now be careful," Mary warned Little Ann. "Think about your wish. There's only one wish apiece."

This didn't bother Little Ann. She had only one wish today. "I want my pumpkin face to win," she said right out as fast as she could.

"You'll never win," Elsie May said. "You can't draw. What a stupid wish."

Phoebe said, "Why don't you just be quiet, Elsie May."

"I want to win the best costume prize." Kate didn't wait to see whose turn was next. She knew what her wish was, and she snatched the lamp from Little Ann.

"You don't even have a costume yet." Elsie May looked disgusted. She thought all these wishes were very dumb. She was going to take her time and think of a really *good* wish. Maybe she would wish to be a famous movie star. Or a famous ballerina. Or have a million dollars.

"I'm going to take my time," she said loudly, looking straight at Kate.

Then Tatty said, "I wonder if the wishes are all used up yet," and that made Elsie May feel nervous. Maybe the other girls would make wishes while she was still deciding, and maybe the one hundred and one wishes would be all used up before she ever had her turn.

"I've changed my mind," Kate said suddenly. "I want to wish something else."

"It's too late, only one wish apiece," Phoebe said.

Kate looked downcast. "I want a goldfish."

"Too late," Phoebe repeated sympathetically.

One wish apiece. Mary closed her eyes and thought hard. She had so many wishes. Wishing for yellow hair instead of red was probably the most important. It was probably her only chance ever to have yellow hair. Or maybe raven black hair would be even better. She had to be abso-

lutely sure before she wished. It would be too late to change her mind afterward.

The room was very quiet for a moment. The lamp was back in the middle of the circle, and the girls who still had wishes to make were thinking hard. Outside it was completely dark now. It was a cold night, a Halloweenish night, with a sliver of moon sailing the black sky over Butterfield Square. Wind rustled in the bare tree branches.

"I wish to be tall," Tatty said suddenly, taking the lamp in her hands. She had been thinking about this all afternoon, even before Miss Lavender found the wishing lamp at the back of the closet. Tatty hadn't been able to reach anything on the closet shelves to help Miss Lavender. At school she couldn't reach the top of the blackboard or the cupboard where the erasers were kept, and she could hardly see out of the school windows unless she got a chair. She wanted to be tall.

"But you *will* be tall when you get older," Phoebe said. "You didn't have to use your wish."

"I want to be tall *now*."

Another dumb wish, thought Elsie May.

All the girls watched Tatty closely, but she did not seem to get any taller.

"You look about the same to me," Kate said finally. They were all disappointed. "Maybe all the wishes are used up."

"Oh, no!" Phoebe moaned dramatically, clutching her heart. "Don't say that Kate! I've just thought of the most wonderful wish anybody could ever think of!"

She seized the lamp from Tatty and held it high.

"I wish to have an invisible cloak," she announced, speaking with assurance and joy. "Whenever I put it on, I will become invisible to all the world."

She set the lamp on the floor and picked up the black velvet cape which lay beside her. "I'll put on my invisible cloak just like this" —with a grand gesture she swept it across her shoulders—"and then I'll be invisible."

Before she had finished speaking, she vanished from sight. The last few words—"and then I'll be invisible"—came from an empty place where Phoebe had been.

5
The Invisible Cloak

No one said anything.

Little Ann's eyes were as big as two big blue china saucers.

Mary and Tatty stared at the place where Phoebe had been.

Kate's mouth dropped open, and Elsie May's skin felt all prickly like when she was cold.

Phoebe was gone—or if not gone, very invisible. Here was proof that the one hundred and one wishes had not yet been all used up, and Phoebe had surely thought of the most wonderful wish anyone could think of.

"Here I am. Over here!" The girls heard a giggling voice from the corner of the room.

They all swung around to look, but no one was there. No one they could see.

"Here I am, here I am," called a voice by the window.

But no one was there.

"Phoebe, please come back." Little Ann was not sure she liked this after all. Tears began to gather in her eyes. "Please come back, Phoebe."

And then Phoebe appeared! She stood in the middle of Tatty's bed, the black velvet cloak crumpled at her feet.

"As soon as I take off my invisible cloak, you can see me again," she exclaimed, radiant with delight. "Isn't it the most marvelous thing!"

Even Elsie May had to admit to herself that having an invisible cloak to use at will was as good a wish as being a famous movie star or famous ballerina or having a million dollars. In Elsie May's opinion, it was the first good wish anybody had made.

"But now you can't be Bat Lady for Halloween," Mary pointed out. "Every time you put on your costume, you'll disappear. No one will see you."

Silence again.

What Mary said was true. Phoebe could not be Bat Lady for Halloween. No one would see her.

"You need another costume," Tatty said helpfully.

Elsie May sighed with disdain. Everybody could see *that*. Phoebe needed another costume.

"What can I be?" Phoebe frowned. She was sorry to give up being Bat Lady, but even being Bat Lady couldn't compare to the fun of being invisible!

"You can have my sheet," Kate said generously. "I want to be something scarier than a ghost anyway."

"What's scarier than a ghost?" Little Ann looked at Kate fearfully.

"I'll be the big green slime monster," Kate said, making a terrible face and waving her skinny arms.

"Suppertime!" a voice shouted at the bedroom door. The girls sitting on the hooked rug by the wishing lamp could hear footsteps in the hall and on the stairs as the other *Good Day* girls trooped down to supper.

The pumpkin pies were cooling on the kitchen counter. Twenty-eight plates were waiting at the dining room table, with places at each end for Miss Lavender and Miss Plum.

"We'd better go," Mary said regretfully. "We haven't got time for any more wishes now."

"Are you going to wear your invisible cloak to supper?" Tatty asked Phoebe as the girls scrambled up.

Before Phoebe could answer, Mary said, "Let's not tell anybody about the lamp until we all have our wishes."

"That's a good idea," Elsie May agreed briskly. "They'll all be wanting turns ahead of us." That would not do.

Tatty put the lamp on the table by her bed, and Elsie May lingered behind as the other girls left the room. She thought she would sneak the lamp into her own bedroom down the hall, just to be on the safe side. She would keep it there until she made up her mind which wish she wanted to make. Other girls might find out about the lamp somehow and make wishes and use them all up before she had her turn.

Kate stuck her head back around the door and called, "Hey, aren't you coming, Elsie May?"

So Elsie May had to go down to supper and leave the lamp behind on Tatty's table—at least for the time being.

All the way downstairs, Elsie May made plans in her head to get back and get that lamp one way or another.

6
Tatty at Suppertime

Soon all the twenty-eight girls were in their places at the dining room table.

Miss Plum was in her chair at one end of the table, and Miss Lavender was in her chair at the other end of the table. There was a good beef stew for supper, and Miss Plum was happy to see all girls present at the table on time and all reasonably neat and tidy.

The next day was Halloween, and as the girls began to eat, there was a buzz and murmur of voices. Everyone was talking about the costume she would wear to school the next day.

Everyone wanted to win the prize for best costume, but what would the prize be? The teachers wouldn't tell, no matter how hard the girls begged.

"It's a silver pen, I bet," one of the girls said, as Cook ladled out the beef stew. "It's always a silver pen."

(One time it had been a silver pen.)

"Onions," Little Ann whispered to Tatty, when she saw the beef stew. Little Ann and Tatty had decided they were not ever going to eat onions in all their whole lives. When the rest of their stew was gone, uneaten onions would be found at the bottom of their bowls.

"How do you know it's a pen?" Kate was the most interested in this news about the prize for best costume. She had wished on the wishing lamp to be the winner. "A silver pen? Are you sure?"

Her question was lost in the hum of voices around the table.

"I heard it was a box of candy," someone else said.

Finally, when it was almost time for the lovely pumpkin pies, Mary looked across the table and saw a strange thing. Tatty's shoulders were even with the back of her chair. Mary looked around the table at the other girls. Everybody looked the same as always. Mary looked back at Tatty. Tatty looked different. Her shoulders were exactly as high as the back of her chair. Her head was sticking up high in the air above the top of her chair. It never had before.

Mary looked down at her plate. She began to eat her pumpkin pie. If Phoebe could be invisible and Tatty was growing taller, then Mary could have yellow hair or black hair instead of red when she made her wish on the wishing lamp.

It was a tremendous thought.

When she had eaten all of her pie, Mary looked at her own reflection in the smooth white plate. She imagined herself with yellow hair, golden hair, the color of dandelions in the summer. Not red.

Mary peeked across the table again to be sure.

Tatty's head was even farther up into the air above the back of her chair.

"I'm going to win the prize for my pumpkin face," Little Ann was telling Miss Plum. Little Ann's place was right beside Miss Plum. She laid her little arms on the table and put her cheek on her arms and smiled up at Miss Plum.

"That's nice," Miss Plum said. She knew that every girl was drawing a jack-o'-lantern face and there was going to be a contest at school and a prize for the best drawing. Miss Plum didn't see how Little Ann could win, but she patted Little Ann's head.

"If it's candy, I'll share," Little Ann promised Miss Plum.

It was time to clear the table. Miss Plum folded her napkin and stood up. Supper was over.

Mary scurried around the table to Tatty's place. She whispered in Tatty's ear, and Tatty's eyes opened like great big owl eyes.

"Really?" Tatty's voice was hushed with awe. Mary put her finger to her lips to keep Tatty quiet.

What Mary whispered to Tatty was, *I think you are growing taller.*

They wanted to be alone to discuss this further, so they went down toward the front end of the hall. No one else went that way. Some of the girls went into the parlor to play by the fireside for awhile. Others went upstairs to look at their costumes one more time or finish homework they had let go until the last minute.

Three girls went with Cook to the kitchen to help with the dishes. It was their turn.

Only Tatty and Mary were at the end of the hall.

Mary opened the hall closet. In the closet were boots and coats, caps and umbrellas. Everything needed to get twenty-eight girls outdoors in snow and rain and cold.

"See if you can reach the shelf," Mary whispered. There was no one to hear, but she whispered anyway.

On the closet shelf were warm knit caps, and Tatty reached up and took down a cap. Then she reached up to the shelf and took down another cap. Now she had two knit caps with pompons, one in each hand.

"You really are taller," Mary whispered. "I always had to get your cap for you. Remember?"

They looked at each other, eye to eye. Yes, eye to eye. Tatty was now as tall as Mary.

"Your wish has come true," Mary said.

It was a splendid moment for Tatty. She was tall, as tall as Mary. At school, she'd be able to reach the top of the blackboard. And next time Miss Lavender cleaned out her closet, Tatty would reach things for her on the shelf.

They hugged each other and jumped around with excitement. "I can have yellow hair." Mary's face was flushed with victory. All her freckles blended together on her pink face.

"Shall we tell Miss Plum and Miss Lavender that I'm taller now?" Tatty wondered, but Mary shook her head.

"Let's wait until they notice. Won't they be surprised!"

"And they'll be surprised when you have yellow hair." Tatty hugged Mary again, and they whispered and giggled and jumped around a little more. Tingling with excitement, they ran upstairs so Mary could make her wish.

Elsie May was one of the girls helping in the kitchen that night, and she was afraid that up in

Tatty's room all the wishes were being used up. Elsie May was in such a hurry to get upstairs, she dropped a plate on the kitchen floor. It broke into a million pieces—at least it seemed like a million pieces to her as she cleaned up the mess.

"Haste makes waste," Cook said.

But Elsie May needn't have worried. When the moment came for Mary to make her wish, she still could not decide whether to wish for yellow hair or black hair. Tatty promised her they would not give the lamp to any of the other girls until Mary had her wish.

"I'll make up my mind by morning for sure," Mary said. She wondered if she could get to sleep with that important decision on her mind.

They were talking about this when Elsie May came bounding up from the land-of-broken-plate. There was the wishing lamp on Tatty's table, but there was no way Elsie May could sneak it away with Tatty, Mary, and Phoebe right there in the room.

"You three better get to bed," Elsie May said, crossly. Maybe *then* she could get the lamp, she thought.

There was the usual amount of chatter and bedtime activity—maybe more chatter than usual because the very next day was Halloween—but by and by Tatty and Mary and Phoebe were snuggling under their covers. When all the lights were out, Elsie May came back to the room.

"Well, is everybody in bed?"

"Of course, we're in bed," Phoebe said. "And we're sound asleep." She began to make funny snoring noises. Mary and Tatty—each in her own little bed—began to giggle in the dark.

"Sleep tight," Elsie May said. She pretended to be very sweet. In the dark she slipped the wishing lamp off Tatty's table and tucked it under her arm. No one saw her; Phoebe was snoring away loudly.

Elsie May took the lamp down the hall to her own bedroom and hid it under her bed so none of the other girls in her room would see it.

In the morning she was going to make her wish. No one would have a chance to get to the lamp before she made her wish to be a famous movie star or a famous ballerina or have a million dollars.

7
Tatty in the Morning

Slowly the dark night passed. The crescent silver moon drifted between the clouds. Then at last the sky began to grow light. The small moon faded. Morning was coming. The streets around Butterfield Square began to grow light and the shadows paled.

It was not quite morning when Tatty woke. It was still half light, half dark in the bedroom.

Mary's bed and Phoebe's bed and the bureau for clothes were only dark shapes in the gloom. The mirror over the bureau was a dusky glimmer.

Usually Tatty was not the first girl to wake up. But she was awake now, and everybody else was still sleeping. She woke feeling very uncomfortable. Her head was pushing against the headboard of her bed, but when she tried to wriggle down further under the covers, her feet bumped into the footboard of the bed. Tatty was filling up her whole bed from head to foot.

"Mary . . . Phoebe . . ."

No one answered.

Tatty pushed back her covers. When she stood up, she felt very cold. Her blue flannel nightgown was way above her knees when it should have been down around her ankles. The sleeves of the nightgown were like the short sleeves of a summer dress—close to Tatty's shoulders, when they should have been down to her wrists.

"M-Ma-Mary . . ." Tatty's voice was trembling now. She felt very big and tall and cold and frightened. And that was a lot of things to feel before the day had even really begun.

"Ph-Ph-Phoebe . . ." Tatty began to shake the closest person, and Phoebe rolled over and opened one eye. When she saw Tatty towering above her, she opened the other eye and sat up with a start.

"Tatty? Is that *you*? What *happened*?" Phoebe's voice was rarely calm, and it certainly was not calm now.

"What's all the fuss?" Mary's sleepy voice faded away as she saw Tatty in the middle of the bedroom, nearly six feet tall in her tiny, little, blue flannel nightgown.

Tatty stood helplessly, her hair tousled from sleeping, her long arms dangling out of her nightgown sleeves, her long legs sticking out below the nightgown hem.

She was a sight to see.

Finally Mary found her voice. "It's like Alice in Wonderland," she said with awe. "Alice found those bottles that said *Drink Me*, remember? And she got little and she got big."

Now that the first shock was over, Phoebe thought it was rather exciting that Tatty was so tall. How much taller would she grow? Alice grew out of a house, arms and legs coming out through

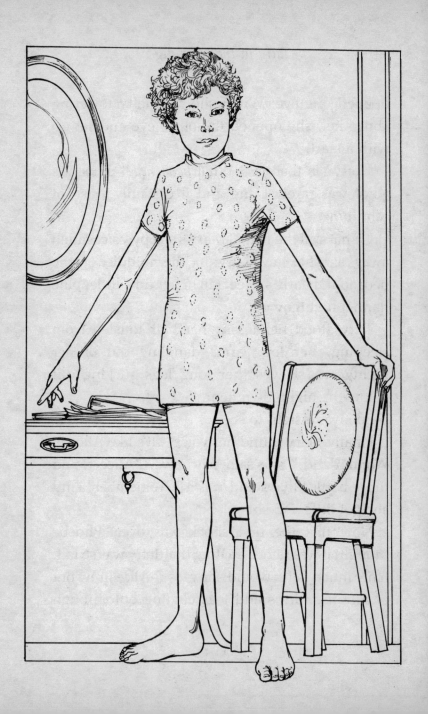

doors and windows. It might be interesting to see if that would happen to Tatty, but then Phoebe had another more practical thought.

"None of her clothes will fit!" she exclaimed. She meant Tatty's clothes, not Alice's. Alice in Wonderland had not had any problems with clothing as she changed sizes, but Tatty surely did. "What will she wear?"

"Oh, what will I wear?" Tatty echoed miserably.

She looked in the mirror, but all she could see was her stomach. Mary and Phoebe looked smaller than she remembered them. Her own feet were far away.

"I don't want to be tall. I want to be my own right size."

"You haven't used *your* wish yet." Phoebe was out of bed now. She stood beside Mary's bed and tugged at Mary's hand. "Get up and wish Tatty back to her right size."

Mary thought about the beautiful yellow hair she was going to have—or beautiful raven black hair. One wish apiece. If she wished for Tatty, her chance for different hair would be lost forever.

"I can't wish," Phoebe said, tugging harder at Mary. "I've already had my wish."

"All right," Mary said bravely. "I'll do it, I'll wish her back to her real, right size."

She knew she must, it was the only thing to do. Good-bye yellow hair or black hair, or whatever color it was to be.

"Quick!" Phoebe whirled around and motioned to Tatty. "Bring the wishing lamp."

Tatty dashed to the table by her bed, but the table was bare. The wishing lamp was gone.

8
Elsie May

Tatty and Mary and Phoebe stared at the empty table by Tatty's bed. Only last night the wishing lamp had been there. Where was it now?

"Someone has stolen our wishing lamp!" Phoebe cried out with astonishment.

"It's gone," Tatty wailed. "Now everybody will see me. Everybody will see how big I am. Everybody will see that my clothes don't fit."

Phoebe had put her marvelous invisible cloak on the chair by her bed. She pulled it off the chair now and said, "Don't cry, Tatty, you can wear this."

Tatty took the cloak and put it around her shoulders. Instantly she vanished from sight. After that, Phoebe and Mary were never sure exactly where Tatty was in the room because they couldn't see her.

"Who took the wishing lamp?" Phoebe looked at Mary. Mary widened her eyes and shook her head; *she* certainly didn't know who had taken the lamp.

"Could it have been Little Ann?" Phoebe asked. Mary shook her head again. "Oh, I don't think so," she said.

Phoebe thought a moment. "I'll bet it was Elsie May."

Mary didn't have time to answer. Elsie May herself opened the bedroom door at that very moment and stood before them, the brass lamp in her hands.

"Elsie May!" Phoebe hissed. "You stole our lamp." She leaped toward the door, but Elsie May held the lamp up high, out of Phoebe's reach.

Although nobody could see where, poor, tall, Tatty was drifting around the room in the invisible cloak.

"You give us that lamp," Mary demanded, frowning fiercely at Elsie May. All her freckles were dark red against the flush of her cheeks.

"You stole our lamp," Phoebe said again, reaching up to try to snatch the wishing lamp away from Elsie May.

"I didn't steal your lamp," Elsie May said. "I just borrowed it overnight, so nobody else could make a wish before I did—if the last wish hasn't already been used by *you-know-who*." Elsie May gave Phoebe a horrid look.

"You always blame me for everything!" This was not exactly true, but Phoebe said it boldly.

"I do not." Elsie May was haughty. She closed the door and came further into the room, holding the lamp.

"I've decided what I want to wish," she announced. "I'm going to wish for a million dollars."

"You can't wish that," Phoebe wailed. "You

have to wish Tatty back to her right size—or give the lamp to Mary so she can wish Tatty back to her right size."

Elsie May stared at Phoebe as if Phoebe were a creature from another planet. "I am going to wish for a million dollars," she repeated firmly.

"I can't wish for Tatty—I've already had my wish. Otherwise *I* would do it!" Phoebe cast herself on Elsie May's mercy. "Oh, please *please*, Elsie May, you're the only one who can save Tatty now. Wish her back to her right size before her head goes straight through the ceiling!"

Elsie May narrowed her eyes and looked at Phoebe. Phoebe was always being so dramatic. Who knew when to trust her? Not Elsie May. She held the lamp closer and looked at Phoebe suspiciously.

"What do you mean, her right size?"

"Her right size, her right size," Phoebe chanted. How could Elsie May be so dumb? "Tatty's wish came true. She got tall—but she got too tall, *way* too tall." Phoebe waved an arm above her head to show how tall Tatty had grown.

Elsie May stared at Phoebe's waving arm. Tatty

was tall now? Phoebe's wish to be invisible had come true, and now Tatty's wish to be tall had come true. More than ever Elsie May wanted her million dollars.

"If I make a wish for Tatty, I won't get my own wish." Elsie May looked back and forth between Phoebe and Mary. She held the lamp with a tighter grip. Nobody was going to get that lamp away from her until she had made her wish.

"Let Mary wish, then." Phoebe made a desperate lunge to try to get the lamp from Elsie May, but Elsie May jerked away.

"Stop that, Phoebe!" she warned. She was beginning to lose her temper.

"Mary hasn't wished yet, let her do it," Phoebe demanded. "Then you can have the lamp back."

"What if it's the last wish," Elsie May snapped. "Then I still won't get *my* wish."

"Who cares! Who cares about your old wish!" Phoebe shouted with exasperation.

"I care!" Elsie May was shouting now too. "It's a million dollars!"

"You're awful!" Phoebe screeched. "You're awful! Don't you care about Tatty?"

"No!"

Phoebe was stunned for only a moment by this dreadful answer. Then, undaunted, she cried out, "Take off the invisible cloak, Tatty, and show Elsie May how you look."

Elsie May certainly wanted to see that. Her jaw dropped with astonishment as Tatty let the invisible cloak slip to the floor and appeared before their eyes (a little taller even than before, Mary thought with dismay).

"Wish her back to her right size. Wish her back! Wish her back!" Phoebe began to chant before Elsie May could collect her wits.

"I wish you would turn into a pumpkin," Elsie May sputtered, and a round orange pumpkin appeared in the spot where Phoebe had been standing.

9
A Dreadful Choice

Downstairs, Cook was setting the breakfast table. Twenty-eight plates, twenty-eight napkins, twenty-eight spoons and cereal bowls. Twenty-eight glasses for milk. Plus plates and cups for Miss Lavender and Miss Plum.

Cook sang to herself as she set the table. She liked to do this. She knew many songs. She could hum and sing every day while she worked and never come to the end of all the songs she knew.

My bonnie lies over the ocean. (spoon, napkin)
My bonnie lies over the sea. (spoon, napkin)
My bonnie lies over the ocean. (bowl, bowl, bowl)
Oh, bring back my bonnie to me.(spoon, napkin)

The table was ready. Just as Miss Lavender and Miss Plum came into the dining room, Cook set a steaming pot of tea by Miss Plum's place at the head of the table. Then Cook went back to the kitchen where the oatmeal was bubbling in a great pot and four pewter milk pitchers were lined up in a row.

Miss Plum sat down in her chair at one end of the table, and Miss Lavender sat next to her. It was really Little Ann's place, the chair next to Miss Plum, but Miss Lavender always sat there early in the morning. She sat there and drank a cup of tea with Miss Plum before the girls came downstairs. When the girls came down for breakfast, Miss Lavender would move to her own place at the other end of the long table.

Miss Plum poured the tea. It fell into the cups in a lovely pale amber stream, piping hot.

"Ah, this looks good," Miss Plum said.

"Indeed, indeed." Miss Lavender bobbed her curly head.

It was a pleasant, peaceful morning. Everything was perfect in Miss Plum's and Miss Lavender's world.

Upstairs, everything was not so pleasant or peaceful. And it certainly wasn't perfect.

"Look what you did!" Mary shrieked at Elsie May when she finally found her voice. At first she had been too startled even to *think*.

Phoebe was gone. Phoebe was a pumpkin.

"Look what you did!" Mary's voice trembled with alarm. All her friends were gone. Tatty wasn't Tatty anymore—not the tiny Tatty that Mary knew. And Phoebe was a pumpkin. Only Elsie May was left. Bossy old Elsie May.

"Well—well—" —Elsie May hunted for words to defend herself—"she made me mad." She stared at the pumpkin rebelliously. "If you would be nicer, Phoebe, these things wouldn't happen," she scolded.

The pumpkin was silent.

Tatty began to cry.

"Give me that!" Mary snatched the wishing

lamp from Elsie May. Something had to be done *right away.* Even Elsie May was a little frightened now. Mary had the lamp, and she was going to wish—but the choice was dreadful. Should she wish for Phoebe or for Tatty? The next wish might be the very last, and no one could ever make any more wishes with the wishing lamp again. Tatty might have to stay a giant forever—or Phoebe might have to stay a pumpkin.

Elsie May twisted the end of a yellow braid. She did not want to get blamed if Phoebe had to stay a pumpkin. "I think you ought to wish Phoebe back," she said carefully. "I don't think Tatty looks so bad."

"This is all your fault," Mary reminded Elsie May, in case she had forgotten.

Tears were streaming down Tatty's cheeks as she shivered in her skimpy nightgown. She drew the velvet cape around her shoulders to keep warm and vanished from view.

"There, see," Elsie May said crossly. "Tatty will be all right. She can put on the invisible cloak, and nobody will know she's too tall."

"She can't stay invisible forever," Mary said.

"She can't go through her whole life being invisible. People will bump into her and sit on her at the movies. They'll never give her anything to eat because they won't know she's there. Nobody will love her."

The room was silent. It was beginning to get lighter outside. Sounds could be heard from the other bedrooms along the hallway. The girls were waking up. Mary and Elsie May looked at each other in desperation. Soon it would be time to go downstairs for breakfast.

"Maybe there are a lot of wishes left," Mary said hopefully, more hopefully than she truly felt. They all knew that there might not be even one single wish left. Miss Lavender and her sister had taken the lamp to school and let everybody have a wish. When Mary thought about that, she felt very nervous.

Tatty was too tall, but maybe they could find some clothes to fit her. Miss Lavender and Miss Plum could make some. Miss Lavender liked to sew. It was worse for Phoebe always to be a pumpkin.

Mary closed her eyes tight. Good-bye yellow

hair, good-bye raven black hair, she thought. Then she spoke clearly like the instructions said to do.

"I wish Phoebe was her real self again."

Before Mary even had her eyes open, she heard a screech of rage. *"Elsie May how could you do that to me!* I wish you were a pumpkin! I wish you were a pumpkin with two heads!"

Phoebe was back! Mary opened her eyes, and it was true. Phoebe was back. There had been at least that one wish left in the lamp. Phoebe's face was pink with fury, her gray eyes flashed. Elsie May went pale, but she didn't turn into a pumpkin with two heads. Phoebe had already used her wish to get the invisible cloak, and the lamp only gave one wish per person.

When Elsie May realized that she wasn't going to change into anything, she pretended she hadn't been worried. "How can a pumpkin have two heads?" she said airily. "That's dumb."

"I don't care." Phoebe was still sputtering with anger. "I wish you were a pumpkin with *six* heads!"

"What about me?" a voice wailed. It was Tatty under her invisible cloak.

"Oh, Tatty!" Phoebe whirled around toward the sound of the voice. "Oh, poor Tatty. We've got to find someone to make a wish for Tatty."

"Maybe all the wishes are gone." Tatty's voice wavered.

"If there are any wishes left, we have to find someone we can trust," Mary said solemnly. She had said good-bye yellow hair, good-bye raven black hair, but maybe other girls wouldn't be so generous. Tatty needed someone who would want her to be her right size as much as Tatty herself wanted it.

"Miss Lavender or Miss Plum," Phoebe said right away. They could be trusted to help Tatty.

Mary shook her head. "Miss Lavender had her wish when she first got the lamp years ago," she reminded Phoebe. "It will have to be Miss Plum."

"She'll be angry at what we did," Elsie May warned everybody. It would be nice to get Tatty back to her right size without having the ladies know what had happened. Elsie May was afraid it would come out that it was she who had turned Phoebe into a pumpkin. She thought Miss Plum and Miss Lavender would not like that.

"We'll get Little Ann to ask Miss Plum," Phoebe said with inspiration. "Miss Plum would never get angry at Little Ann."

The other girls thought this was a good idea. Phoebe hurried off to get Little Ann. Little Ann was dressing, and Phoebe came back dragging her by the hand, one shoe off and one shoe on. While Little Ann sat on the floor and put on her other shoe, Mary knelt beside her and gave her the directions.

"All you have to say is, 'Please, Miss Plum, wish Tatty back to her right size.' Can you remember that?"

Little Ann nodded. Elsie May rolled her eyes to the ceiling. She was sure Little Ann would get it all wrong. Getting Little Ann was a mistake.

Mary carried the lamp and they all went downstairs. Tatty came along too, but nobody could see her in the invisible cloak. "Are you still here?" Phoebe kept whispering, and Elsie May nearly tripped over the invisible cloak when she walked too close to Tatty.

None of the other girls had come downstairs yet. Miss Plum and Miss Lavender were still sitting at the table by the teapot. In the kitchen Cook was still singing to herself as she stirred the oatmeal. The kitchen windows were decorated with Halloween pictures the girls had drawn for Cook. Beyond these windows, decorated with witches on broomsticks and various terrible monsters, Halloween morning was growing lighter and lighter.

"She'll get it wrong, I bet," Elsie May whispered to Phoebe as they reached the dining room doorway and Mary put the lamp into Little Ann's hands.

"Well, look who's here." Miss Lavender looked up from her tea when she heard footsteps and whispering in the doorway.

Little Ann came into the room, carrying the wishing lamp carefully in her small hands.

The other girls clustered by the door. Mary crossed her fingers for good luck and held her breath.

Was there one more wish left?

"Please, Miss Plum," Little Ann said softly, setting the lamp in Miss Plum's thin lap, "wish Tatty back to her right size."

10
Miss Know It All

Miss Plum held the wishing lamp in her hands. She looked at Little Ann with surprise. Then she looked toward the door where Mary and Phoebe and Elsie May were clumped together in a huddle.

"Wish Tatty back to her right size?" Miss Plum turned back to Little Ann. "I don't understand. Where is Tatty? Has something happened?"

Mary came forward loyally. "She's big, Miss Plum. Very big. She wished on the wishing lamp."

Miss Lavender clasped her hands, somewhat

atingle at the news. After all, it was her wishing lamp, and she was responsible for whatever happened.

"Show them, Tatty." Mary spoke toward the doorway where Phoebe and Elsie May were standing. Suddenly Tatty appeared beside them—*towered* beside them with her long arms and her long cold legs. It was a sight to behold. Miss Lavender thought she might faint, and Miss Plum was so startled she was at a loss for words— which rarely ever happened. A thousand thoughts flew through her mind at once: Some dreadful fate had befallen dear little Tatty. Should a doctor be called? Should Tatty be hurried back to bed? Was she still growing?

"Oh, I wish Miss Know It All were here," Miss Plum blurted out, and once again Miss Lavender felt faint. *At that very moment Miss Know It All appeared beside the dining room table.* Whatever corner of the world she came from, evidently she had still been in bed when she was summoned by Miss Plum. She appeared complete with a long blue nightgown and a number of pink hair rollers in her hair.

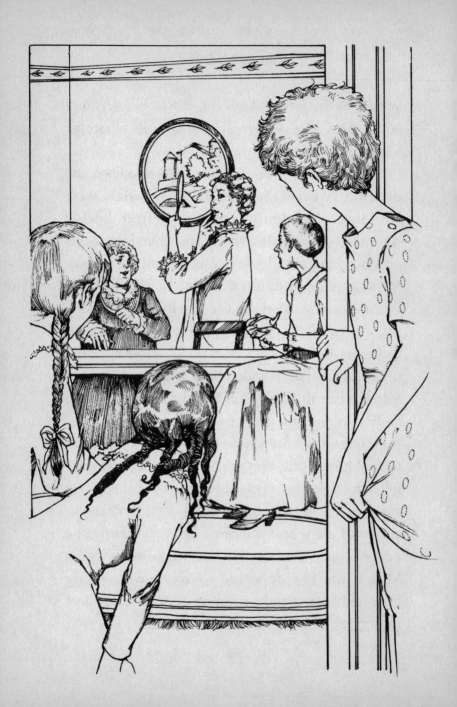

The girls were thrilled to see Miss Know It All; they all loved her dearly. She knew just about everything there was to know, and whenever she visited Butterfield Square, she answered all their questions and told them interesting things they had always wondered about, like why stars twinkle and how to make invisible ink. She had eighty-seven cures for hiccups and a box of chocolate candy that never ever got empty, no matter how much was eaten.

Now here she was again! Miss Plum had wished for her.

"You used your wish!" Phoebe shouted out. "Miss Plum used up her wish!"

Another wish was gone, and Tatty was still a giant.

Miss Know It All rubbed her eyes sleepily and gazed around with surprise. "Why, I'm in Butter-field Square. I'm at *The Good Day Orphanage For Girls*."

Tatty drew the cloak around herself again to keep warm, vanishing, and all the girls gathered around Miss Know It All. But their joy in seeing

Miss Know It All was shattered by a terrible racket at the front door.

Bang, bang, bang, bang. They shuddered. They all knew the sound of that knock.

Miss Lavender and Miss Plum looked at each other in surprise, and then Miss Lavender remembered. "He's come back for his gloves," she said, nodding to Miss Plum. Then she looked toward the girls. "Elsie May, you may open the door."

Elsie May stalked off, muttering, "Why does it always have to be me?" It was one of her favorite sayings.

Other girls were beginning to come downstairs for breakfast. They crowded the hallway as Mr. Not So Much stepped in. Elizabeth, Nonnie, Cissie, Sue, tomboy Kate. Dark blue dresses moved like waves of the ocean around Mr. Not So Much as he strode after Elsie May toward the dining room.

"Good morning, ladies," he said, announcing himself at the dining room door. His long bony face was as stern as ever. It was also slightly red with cold. Outside a strong wind was blowing.

"Out so early?" Miss Lavender asked meekly. She hoped Mr. Not So Much wouldn't notice Miss Know It All standing there in her nightgown.

But of course he did. It was the first thing he noticed.

"Who is this?" he demanded, not recognizing Miss Know It All with her hair rolled up.

"Why, it's Miss Know It All," Miss Plum said, her head still spinning at this amazing result to her wish. "You remember her, Mr. Not So Much."

Mr. Not So Much took a closer look. Yes, he thought the woman did look somewhat familiar. But she seemed oddly dressed for a visit. He gave her a brief, unfriendly nod, and addressed himself to Miss Plum again. "I always take a constitutional before breakfast," he said. "I was in the neighborhood, and I thought I would get the gloves I left here yesterday."

"Of course." Miss Plum was about to ask one of the girls to run to the parlor and get the gloves when Mr. Not So Much caught sight of the wishing lamp in Miss Plum's lap.

"Are you people still fussing with that foolish thing?" Mr. Not So Much demanded.

By now other girls were clustered by the dining room doorway, whispering about Miss Know It All, whom they were all quite surprised to see. Mr. Not So Much included everybody in a frown of disapproval. "There is too much foolishness here," he said, reaching for the lamp.

But Phoebe was too quick for him. She seized the lamp from Miss Plum and pushed it into Miss Know It All's hands.

"Please, Miss Know It All, wish Tatty back to her right size!"

"I will indeed," Miss Know It All said, wide awake now and knowing all she needed to know, which in her case was everything.

"I wish Tatty back to her right size," she said without hesitation.

There was a long moment of silence. Phoebe thought she would burst. Mary's fingers ached from being crossed so tightly for luck. She could hardly stand the suspense. It was as though clocks stopped, time stood still, the globe of the world stopped turning.

Finally, the old black velvet cape slid to the floor

in a heap and there stood Tatty. Little Tatty. Tatty at her own size. Not quite tall enough to reach the shelves in the closets or the cookie jar in the kitchen or the top of the blackboard at school. Just her own right size. Her nightgown was down to her ankles; the sleeves were down to her wrists.

Mary and Phoebe began to jump up and down, shouting, "There was a wish left! There was a wish left!"

Even Elsie May smiled. "Hi, shrimp," she said, patting Tatty's head.

Little Ann took a sugar lump from the white dish by the teapot and popped it into her mouth. Everybody was happy.

Happiest of all was Tatty herself. "Oh, thank you, Miss Know It All, thank you!" Tatty began to jump around and clap her hands and other girls began to join in.

This was entirely too much noise and confusion for Mr. Not So Much. He had no idea what was going on or why Miss Know It All was in her nightgown—or why she was even present at all. It was time the nonsense stopped.

"Wishing lamp! Wishing lamp!" he muttered, snatching the lamp from Miss Know It All. "I wish I was home having my breakfast."

All the girls pictured Mr. Not So Much home at his table, his hat on his head, his napkin tucked under his chin, a fork in one hand, a knife in the other.

What would he eat for breakfast? Surely it would not be anything very tasty or anything very much. They knew he did not approve of spending money for anything.

Phoebe thought his breakfast might be some skimpy vegetables grown in his garden at no cost. Radishes, perhaps.

Mary thought of a single thin piece of toast, lying alone on a plate without butter or jam.

Tatty couldn't imagine Mr. Not So Much eating anything.

I wish I was home having my breakfast. Mr. Not So Much had made a wish—his wish—but he did not vanish from the room. The lamp had not taken him home to his breakfast table. The sound of his words died away, and there he still stood, holding the brass lamp.

The wishes were all used up.

Everyone stared at Mr. Not So Much. Twenty-eight little girls and three ladies, one in a nightgown. Four, counting Cook who had just arrived with the milk pitchers.

"As long as you're not home eating breakfast," Miss Plum said when it became certain that Mr. Not So Much's wish would not be granted, "perhaps you would like to have breakfast with us."

The pitchers wobbled in Cook's hands. Mr. Not So Much stay for breakfast? He was sure to say there was too much milk on the oatmeal and too much jam on the muffins. Her lovely breakfast would be spoiled by his constant complaints.

To her relief, Cook heard Mr. Not So Much say, "No, thank you. I'll just have my gloves and be on my way."

Miss Know It All, on the other hand, said she would be happy to stay for breakfast as long as she was there.

Elsie May ran off to get the gloves, closely followed by Phoebe and a whole string of girls.

"Not so much commotion," Mr. Not So Much

called after them, although he knew it was of little use. No one at *The Good Day* had an ounce of sense that he could see.

Finally, when Mr. Not So Much had his gloves and was gone, Mary and Tatty and Phoebe got together in a huddle.

"So that was the last wish, the one Miss Know It All made about Tatty. It was the absolutely last wish." Mary's voice was full of awe.

"The very last wish!" Phoebe clasped her hands dramatically and waved her head from side to side. "Otherwise, Tatty, you would have grown right on through the ceiling."

Then they discussed what a "constitutional before breakfast" was. Mr. Not So Much had said he always took one.

"It's probably a pill, like a vitamin or something," Mary said.

"Maybe it's a special kind of bath," Phoebe said.

Tatty thought it was a bus or a train.

When they asked Miss Know It All, she said a constitutional was a walk taken as exercise.

Elsie May who had overheard, said, "I knew that all the time," to show how smart she was.

11
All's Well

"All's well that ends well," Miss Lavender said, patting her curls. The twenty-eight girls were at their places around the table. The oatmeal and muffins were delicious and everybody ate hungrily.

Miss Lavender had given Miss Know It All a dress to wear. Miss Know It All was not as plump as Miss Lavender so there was more dress than was needed, but Miss Know It All did look quite charming amid the ruffles. She was going home after breakfast, and she needed the dress for the trip. She would have to go by train, as there were no more wishes to whisk her around.

"Yes, all's well," Miss Plum agreed. She smiled at everyone. "All's well that ends well."

Elsie May, who had not gotten to make her wish to have a million dollars, didn't think that all had ended well at all.

Nor did Mary. "I didn't get to wish for yellow hair," Mary told Miss Plum. "Or maybe black."

Miss Plum looked shocked. "You were going to wish for yellow hair? Or black hair?"

Mary nodded. "Yes, I was. I'm tired of red hair."

"Mary," Miss Know It All said, "your red hair is your crowning glory. You wouldn't want to wish away your crowning glory."

Mary stirred her oatmeal and looked at Miss Know It All. She had never thought of her curly red hair as her crowning glory. Maybe it was good that she still had it after all.

When the girls came home for lunch that afternoon, they put on their Halloween costumes. There was going to be a costume parade at school, and a prize for the best costume.

"That will be me," Kate reminded everybody.

She had wished for the prize with the wishing lamp.

"That will be a true miracle," Elsie May said, turning up her nose at Kate's costume.

Kate had waited until the last minute to choose her costume, and all the best masks and dress-up clothes were already taken. She was disappointed not to find anything that would change her into a big green monster. She found nothing better than an old skeleton suit nobody else wanted and a tattered witch wig that was too big and nearly covered her whole face.

"You have no face," Little Ann said with concern when Kate appeared in her costume.

When the girls went back to school and the bustle and confusion died down, Cook found Miss Lavender's old black velvet cape in a corner. "Oh, that's for the rummage sale," Miss Lavender said. Cook put the cape in the rummage sale box. No one at *The Good Day Orphanage For Girls* ever saw it again. Phoebe's heart was broken. And somewhere there is an invisible lady who bought a cape at a rummage sale.

After school, Kate came home with the prize for

the best costume—a silver pen. Little Ann won the prize for the best jack-o'-lantern face. Her prize was a candle shaped like a golden pumpkin. They had won, just as they had wished.

Cook made taffy apples for the girls to eat.

As the afternoon darkened, the ghosts and goblins, pirates and witches and devils, three black cats (who were really Tatty, Mary, and Little Ann), one skeleton, and one gypsy princess with yellow braids, sat on the floor and on chairs around the parlor and ate taffy apples.

Cook brought in the last surprise, a great pumpkin carved into a grinning face, lighted inside with a fat candle. She put it right in the center of the parlor windowsill, and all the girls had to run out into the yard to see how the pumpkin looked from outside.

After the girls went back indoors, the pumpkin shone in the window for a long time on the cold, dark Halloween night.

Miss Plum set the wishing lamp on the mantle as a memento of events—and as a reminder to Tatty that when you are seven years old, it is all right to be not very tall.

About the Author

CAROL BEACH YORK is a writer with over forty juvenile and young adult books to her credit, including the popular Bantam titles MISS KNOW IT ALL, MISS KNOW IT ALL RETURNS, THE GOOD DAY MICE and ON THAT DARK NIGHT.

Born and raised in Chicago, she began her career writing short stories and sold her first one to *Seventeen* magazine. Her first teen novel, a romance, SPARROW LAKE, was published in 1962. Since then she has contributed many stories and articles to magazines in both the juvenile and adult markets, in addition to her activity as a novelist. She especially enjoys writing suspense stories.

Ms. York lives in Chicago with her daughter, Diana.